# RISQUÉ AND FRISKY

## VOLUME I

BY
AIYSHA SWALLOWGREN

ISBN 978-0-9984840-5-1
First Printing July 2022
Printed in United States of America

# Contents

# ADDICTION

I say dive head first into your addiction
There's nothing wrong with being a sexy vixen
I'll hold the space and carefully listen
You dance and as you sweat and glisten
I say give into pleasure, give into intuition
There's a picture of you by sexy, you're the definition
Of sexbomb and I'll always happily mention
How divine you are and let's explore our addiction
Together today let's become magicians
Making magic and light that's a great addiction
I write this to bring forth to fruition
Let's make having pleasure a competition
I have a confession, I make this admission
You make my heart sing like a famous musician
Giving you unlimited pleasure is my mission
Give into temptation, give into your addiction

# AGENT PROVOCATEUR

I desire to see you dressed in Agent Provocateur
You're absolutely sensation I mean your
Body is like cocaine to me totally pure
Wiggle your hot ass I need more
Baby you're so sexy wearing Agent Provocateur
Face down ass up I'm licking you on the floor
Making you think and do things most impure
You love my filthy tongue and when I call you a whore
You keep soaking me with your feminine allure
I'm licking every crevice and contour
Of your body to ensure
That you stay wet I'll always savor
When you let me lick you through your Agent Provocateur

# ALL TRUST

He knew how to give her all trust
He'd always protect her she just
Needs to relax and allow his lust
To overwhelm her she cussed
Nothing gets her wet like all trust
He was firm, he was gentle, and he never rushed
He knew how to pleasantly please her bust
On a hot day he lifted her skirt like a gust
Of cool air she reads this while he brushed
Her hair and she happily discussed
How she fantasized about his thick thrust
Making her body slowly erupt
He made her see stars, he's her stardust
She dressed as a maid and started to dust
No panties today, just all trust

# ALONE

I want you to read this while you are alone
Tonight I'm whispering to you like Romeo
I want to fill you with pleasure starting to slow
Kisses on your neck I want to make you moan
And look in the mirror and take pictures with your phone
Tonight you are being served on a throne
You have such lovely eyes and cheekbones
You are more precious than any gemstone
Greatest mother and artist ever that's what's going on your tombstone
All your fears and insecurities will be overthrown
I'm touching you in your many erogenous zones
I want you to enjoy your body while you are alone
You've got the sexiest figure, so beautiful and tone
I will keep you free and never try to control or own
You I only ask for consent, my actions I want you to condone
It's our little dirty secret, for you and I alone

# ANGEL

She's doing her best to corrupt this angel
She's bending purposefully showing her angles
Opening a few buttons her breasts dangle
She smiles like you ever been to hell
It's hot and fun she watches me swell
She's curious what I'd do if she fell
In my lap with her hips creating a spell
She bent over and I could smell
Her excitement like wait I'm an angel
Her body is covered in glittery gel
Angel do you want me to give you the hard sell
She wants millions of this angel's cells
She grinds her hips and whispers I won't tell
Anyone if you sin with me sweet angel

# ANIMATED

She gets really worked up and animated
When I whisper things XXX rated
She's my teacher and she has educated
Me very well, she's always fascinated
With my creations, I verbally illustrated
Her touching herself and she's highly animated
She's my Julia Roberts so I compensated
Her very well and she's well lubricated
She screams you keep me so motivated
To touch myself I carefully calculated
How many times I orchestrated
Her orgasms, how many times I stimulated
Her and she always feels appreciated
I whisper you are so sexy and sophisticated
Getting her to touch herself is uncomplicated
She's totally captivated and intoxicated
She's completely soaked, totally saturated
The important of good foreplay can't be overstated
After reading this I know where her hand will be located

# ANTICIPATION

She couldn't help herself, the anticipation
Of him touching her with his imagination
He slowly explored her, his fascination
With pleasing her made her give into temptation
She couldn't stop herself and the vibration
In her panties caused excessive perspiration
He whispered you're the most beautiful creation
Her mind and body awash in elation
He knew she would start a slow rotation
Of her hips, he greatly increased her circulation
All her nerve endings stimulated from conversation
She couldn't muffle her gleeful exclamation
He got her off with sweet anticipation

# APPRECIATION

You deserve adoration and appreciation
I want to be one of the very few men
That understand what creates a sexy fascination
How can I tonight make you experience elation
I'll give you the most pleasurable sensations
Let my tongue express my appreciation
Is this hot enough to cause dehydration
I want you at the peak of your ovulation
My tongue touches the spot responsible for temptation
Can I be the source of your masturbation
All you need is genuine love and affirmations
Let my tongue take you beyond celebration
Are these words totally the best combination
I know how hard you occupation
Is and how rare it is to receive generous appreciation

# ASSISTANT

I dreamt of being your personal assistant
At first you were a bit hesitant
But I assured you I'd give it a hundred percent
Working with you is fabulous torment
The first time filing you slowly bent
Over and winked it was no accident
Your body is firm and now my mind's cement
I grabbed some files to hide the tent
You created, I'm a perverted assistant
This year Santa for my present
I'd like her to make hot content
With me her outfits truly invent
New levels of depravity, the extent
Of which causes my energy to be pent
Up like her hot skirt just went
Higher and she gave her consent
To take sexy photos, she laughed at the indent
In the file and said you're a great assistant
Get under my desk, she was insistent
She said now you know your assignment
I'm her assistant, inhaling her scent

# Bashfulness

She said please accept my bashfulness
And I was like sure as I looked up her dress
You keep being bashful and I will confess
The many ways I desire to see you slowly start to undress
Picturing a windy day and you in a thin sundress
Guess what I'm doing right now, guess
I'm massaging your brain with total access
We're like children and today at recess
She started being a little less bashful, she started to press
Against me slowly and I was like do you feel my bashfulness
You'd turn me on wearing no makeup in sweats
I'd really enjoy seeing you in nice fishnets
Today when let's surrender to the process
I'll never ask for commitment or try to possess
You are always treated lovingly, patiently, with niceness
Come sit in my lap and let's discuss bashfulness
We'll talk about the first thing that pops up let's obsess
On how we can make light and how we can bless
Each other thank heavens for your bashfulness

# BATHING

Make a wish she said I said see her bathing
Now there's a patience test I'm patiently waiting
Picturing your cute little hips gyrating
Do you know little princess what you are making
Me into you've created a monster, I have such a craving
To listen to you while bathing
Your voice is like music and you are aging
Perfectly getting better with time you are amazing
Seriously the anger in my heart you are replacing
With joy and you ignited a passion that never quit blazing
I'm so curious to watch you shaving
Show me your world my favorite plaything
I'm so weak, I'm once again caving
Into lust dreaming of you bathing

# BIKING

She looks so good happily biking
Her cool gold hat nicely shining
Beauty with no clothes that's striking
I'm a lightning rod and she is lightning
She's the hottest naked cycling
I don't know if there's anything more exciting
She is an inspiration and I'm writing
Surely someone should start describing
That she's smoking hot and I'm piping
Hot watching her biking
I hope this is to her liking
Wearing nothing and happily smiling
She is nude and I'm highlighting
Her assets, her stock isn't the only thing rising
Writing to make her laugh like I'm dying

# BLOSSOM

It's an honor to hold space while you blossom
The leaves of change are falling like it's autumn
It's an honor to remind you how awesome
You are and how you are so special and uncommon
Somebody has to remind you that you have a great bottom
Mentally I massage you and your tension starts to become less often
Meanwhile I'm over here like a coffin
Wait I mean you've made me as stiff as a board I can't soften
I remind you of your greatness when you've forgotten
You're the loveliest flower in full blossom

# BOOTY CALL

I just got an interesting booty call
She's got such a perfect and small
Heart shaped booty I want it all
She's a schoolgirl skipping down the hall
I stop her and push her against the wall
It gets her so wet like rainfall
She's under my desk and starts to crawl
She shows me her butt for me to draw
She's a naughty schoolgirl, a horny doll
She's a perfect ten and my bowling ball
Fingering her softly she's my waterfall
She loves my protection, I'm so tall
She's calling again, my hot booty call

# Breast Friend

She's not my best friend, she's my breast friend
Really you wanna see them again
You really, truly enjoy seeing my tits she sins
I can't stop admiring how thin
You are when you bend
Over my cock twitches breast friend
Thanks for not making me pretend
That I'm not really turned on when
You pull them out I never offend
Her by saying when you send
Me sexy photos I start to extend
Stick out your tongue breast friend
You've also got a great rear end

# BUST

I woke up this morning dreaming of your bust
I know you have a fabulous bust
I tried to stop touching myself to you and I just
Can't seem to stop thinking of when you cussed
Fucking you said over and over my mind will combust
You make me the horniest, you create such lust
Between us there is so much love, so much trust
I want to give it to you nice and slow, never rushed
Let me worship your body, starting with your bust

# CATNIP

Being treated sweetly was her catnip
Being respected make her shake her hips
She's wearing La Perla and starts to unzip
Being spoiled makes her start to strip
Whoa she just started to rip
My shirt off this might be as hot as it gets
She's licking me like I'm catnip
She starts to lovingly lick
My body, in my mouth she shoves her tit
The way I honor her makes her drip
She starts to sink onto my tip
Then quickly she starts to slip
Further on me with the tightest grip
I grab her and easily flip
Her onto my face I cum equipped
She's dripping all over my face as I happily sip
Her juices are my form of catnip

# CHEESECAKING

She could really go for some cheesecaking
He massaged her feet firmly aiding
Her relieving stress, easing her aching
When his mouth started fixating
On her feet it was truly groundbreaking
She melted in his mouth, yummy chessecaking
She closed her eyes and was waiting
For his hands to move higher he's taping
Her mouth shut and his fingers are gyrating
Right on her clit he's fucking breaking
All the rules and his tongue is bathing
Her as he increased the speed of his vibrating
She smiled as her juices started escaping
His touch and patience was so titillating
His devotion to her pleasure was fascinating
He fed her Godiva cheesecake while she's masturbating
Fuck yes, more delicious cheesecaking

# CHERRY PIE

I want to taste your sweet cherry pie
I'm slowly with my tongue parting your thighs
My goodness sir I
Don't know why I can't stay dry
But I like the huge bulge could I try
To sit in your lap and jump really high
Land on my dick why don't you lie
Back and let me lick your sweet cherry pie
Let me make you so wet you can't deny
The puddle pooling and I'm the reason why
You can't stop touching yourself, I'm that guy
I'm very sweet, I'm very timid, and I'm super shy
I'll do anything to taste your sweet cherry pie

# CLASSIC

A toast to classic beauty, here's to the classic
Women like you make opportunities from the tragic
You are bold, you are fearless, you are fantastic
You are the bomb, that's why you're bombastic
You keep it real, most people are plastic
But you my dear are a sensational classic
Wherever you walk you stop traffic
Asking how does it get better that that it's magic
Today lay back and let's explore beyond fantastic
You love my sweetness my favorite tactic
Is to build up to do something very dramatic
I want to please you, I want to make you spastic
Dancing together our souls move beyond ecstatic
I'm your biggest fan, I'm a fanatic
Let my words in your body cause gymnastics
Today I'm going down the rabbit hole like Alice
Wait I mean I'm going down on you like the Titanic
Just keeping it classy, this guy's a classic

# CLOTHING

She said be my boyfriend and she started removing her clothing
He objected saying I really want you to imagine slowing
3Down and mentally enjoy where this is going
I'm slowly starting to lick your mind, the feelings are flowing
I give you tons of small kisses to get you glowing
It's a different kind of sexiness I am proposing
It's not your body that I want to see you exposing
Though wonderful I want your hands to start roaming
Lay back and listen to what I am composing
Biting your lip and really hoping
That someone could actually enjoy and appreciate you with clothing
You have very sexy everything, I'm not joking
I want to make you really start moaning
Imagining me licking your neck, we begin molding
Together as one I help you feel light, it's engrossing
You and as I embrace you it feels like floating
I'll lick your back slowly until you start moaning
Has anyone ever made you leak through your clothing

# CONFIDENT

She loved that he made her feel confident
When he said she was sexy he really meant
It and she enjoyed his response when she sent
Him racy photos she gave it one hundred percent
What helped her most was his intent
He praised her body and made her more confident
He was such a flirtatious, polite gent
When he shared with her how his energy was pent
Up she purposefully and happily bent
Over texting him do I make a tent
She mailed him a package to share her scent
She knew how to quickly make cement
She enjoyed being totally confident

# CREAMING

I love when you get so excited you start creaming
I want to drink your juices as I slowly start eating
You making you feel so hot like you are needing
To explode I will make you see colors like you are dreaming
I want to get you hot, I want you overheating
I want you to touch yourself until you start screaming
Fuck yes sir, you are why I am creaming
I want to make you so happy you start weeping
You deserve a man that is devoted to pleasing
Your wildest fantasies imagine my hands creeping
Along your lower back as I whisper you love creaming
Don't you filthy slut I enjoy keeping
You on the edge of your seat with a puddle from your leaking
I treat you like a queen and when you are queening
That's when you start uncontrollably creaming

# DESIRE

You fill my mind with passionate desire
I want to write to make our vibe higher
Let me find your passion and be the lighter
Burning hot delicious desire
She loved hearing she was able to inspire
Allow me to be your pleasure multiplier
You're so fit and your pussy couldn't be any tighter
My tongue is on your body and it's like an electric wire
Pulsating pleasure and increasing your desire
Generous men that know just how to admire
You get you super horny little devil says I require
Many more licks you've started a wildfire
I'm an innocent dear and you are a fierce tiger
I'll sing your praises daily like I'm in choir
Singing let me create an unquenchable desire

# DESK

He was laying down under her desk
She moaned as his strong hands pressed
Firmly on her toes she growls you're the best
She was studying totally undressed
Giving him a real eyeful under her desk
His hands in cuffs under arrest
His tongue was rarely allowed to rest
She groaned he had just messed
Up her concentration he confessed
He loved helping relieve her stress
She leaned back saying I suggest
You lick my asshole he didn't protest
Her pleasure, her needs, he was obsessed
He met her needs, especially the unexpressed
Ones, he's happily serving under her desk

# Discrete

She could always count on him to be discrete
He'd gladly and watch her eat
Out her beautiful friend he's so neat
And polite keeping her secrets was no small feat
She was a truly certified freak
Her and her female friends make each other leak
He gets access to it all because he's ultra-discrete
She loves wearing super high heels on her feet
Wearing expensive lingerie bringing absolute heat
Occasionally they'd feel that they were incomplete
He got to enjoy their tricks and treats
When it comes to discretion nobody can compete
He was generous, kind, and always super sweet
They reward him with vials of their essence that they'd secrete
She's friends with porn stars, rockstars, and some athletes
He was granted access to the world's hottest models, the wealthy, the elite
Because they all knew he was the champion of remaining discrete

# DONUT GREASE

She wanted a partner that was hotter than donut grease
She wanted lust that would never cease
He told her that she was his most favorite piece
When he whispers to her she experiences peace
His tongue was her ultimate release
He covered her body in kisses hotter than donut grease
He lays her on the table, she's his centerpiece
His appetite for her will never decrease
Her excretions taste like hot donut grease
Tonight on her body he will truly feast
She's his beauty and he's her vulnerable beast

# DUET

Our bodies are singing a magical duet
I tied her down and made her my pet
Her body is shaking, she is starting to fret
She's dripping in anticipation how naughty I'll get
I'm going to do things, let's make a bet
I'll bet I can lick every drop of your sweat
Ladies first is big dick energy mindset
If you serve ladies they'll never forget
When they are crying and super upset
Tell them they're more beautiful than a Maui sunset
Then use your tongue to do the whole alphabet
You're the sexiest and I perfectly reflect
Your naughtiness, we make a sexcellent duet

# Embracing

Twenty more pounds on her she's embracing
It and I'm over here like wow, amazing
She's out of this world sexy and I'm spacing
Out twenty more pounds of lusciousness I'm gazing
At my curvy friend like wow I'm never complaining
About your body at any weight I'll be raving
Your body is a temple and I'm praising
Imagining me on my knees but I'm not praying
I'm her naughty secret, her private plaything
Under her desk she can't help but playing
With me I am slowly grazing
On her and my mouth is embracing
Her body, his tongue is generously bathing
Her extra weight and getting her blazing
Hot she touches her body, quickly embracing

# Empower

Vulnerability shows strength and power
Water their souls and watch them flower
What an honor it is to be allowed to empower
The most beautiful women increasing their horsepower
They said your sweetness is like gunpowder
I never had someone try to overpower
Me but she just ripped off my trousers
And said you have very sexy brainpower
I can't believe my friend tried to deflower
Me she said feel to join me in the shower
I laugh I'm too timid, I'm a coward
I said let me praise you a little louder
I'm just here to support and empower
She asked me to record while she showered

# ENDURE

She appreciated his patience, he was willing to endure
She said please be patient and he said sure
He built her up, it was his honor to reassure
Her that she was the sexiest, she had the most allure
While he waited she gave him a special tour
Of her closet and said why don't we explore
My lingerie section and instantly his mind filled with fervor
She trusted him, she knew her safety was secure
He treated her like royalty so he received the grand tour
She said lick me please, slow licks and make sure
You spend lots of time slowly kissing me I know you're
Excited but be patient and know that your
Pleasure is of paramount importance more sweetness more
She didn't know how much more pleasure her body could endure

# EVERYTHING

She wants a lion, a wild king
She would let the right man do anything
She wants him to powerfully fling
Her around like a little girl he makes her swing
In circles the one thing about Daddy is he can bring
Out the nastiest, sluttiest parts of her everything
She's ever dreamed of doing he tied her with string
She loved his slaps it made her ears ring
Daddy made it so wet, then he would sting
Her in the ass back in your mouth, you said everything

# EXOTIC

You dear are so very exotic
Your eyes are absolutely hypnotic
You get me higher than my chronic
I'm crazy and a tad bit psychotic
But the cause is women that are extra exotic
Your beauty is stronger than any narcotic
For you I've got jokes, I'll be a comic
What's the difference between erotic and exotic
There is none you belong laying in the tropics
Pleasing women specifically you is my favorite topic
How can I make you shine like supersonic
I'll do anything to excite someone so exotic

# EXPLAIN

Her gratitude to me was hard to explain
I put happiness right into her vein
She had never felt like someone's main
Priority, it eased and erased lots of pain
I am a lion and my colorful mane
Built her trust back up, it's hard to explain
I was like a medicine for a migraine
Being treated lovingly tastes like Veuve champagne
She feels so good it makes her brain
Explode and her panties start to rain
She showed me that I made a wet stain
She said you're profound and profane
Her arousal is becoming impossible to contain
Showing him without words made it easy to explain

# EXPLORE

He encourage her to really explore
Her secret desires to be a total whore
She dreamt of being pushed to the floor
Her beautiful, expensive dress he tore
Off her and it made her wetter than ever before
She wanted to be taken on all fours
She wanted to be used fully and left sore
He gave her pleasure and pain galore
Safely they developed sensual rapport
She shuddered as his tongue entered her backdoor
Reading this got her so hot she can't ignore
He was a sexual beast and he made her roar
Who knew angles could be this hardcore
His directness made her totally adore
That it was safe to freely explore

# EXPOSE

She said what would happen if you chose
To bravely and repeatedly expose
Your heart, let's see how that goes
She laid back and started to pose
Slowly she starts removing her clothes
Snow she's wearing a smile and pantyhose
Gleefully she demands me now compose
For me a new poem that shows
Me how what you feel as I expose
I'm creating dew drops on her rose
She said make sure everyone knows
That a man that listens and slows
Down knows how to make me glow
She's on fire and I'm her hose
I'm inhaling her with my nose
She huskily says I propose
That you make our bodies superimpose
She allows to safely and boldly expose

# EXQUISITE

He made her dreams sexually exquisite
The absolute care for her heart he'd visit
Quietly whispering you're so exquisite
He showed her the best etiquette
The evidence of his treatment was evident
In her dreams he pleases her in exquisite
Way when she's feeling very pessimistic
He compliments her often, his mystic
Nature and his sweetness was an excellent
Aphrodisiac her heart was so delicate
His tongue on her body felt like velvet
He knew how to get her in her element
She deserves worship, he's so affectionate
He was her sensual healing specialist
Tonight in her dreams he's especially exquisite

# Eye

I dream of looking at you eye to eye
I wake you up slowly licking your inner thighs
You giggle and I'm like do you know why
I never ask about if you have a boyfriend or some guy?
It's because I only desire to apply
Love to you and lift you up to the sky
It's not that I want to say goodbye
It's just that I love watching you leave go fly
On a private plane to Kauai
I never ask if there are other men nearby
Because all it does is make me cry
I'll never experience that, hideous am I
I wish you'd have them take pictures looking spry
With them in your mouth I wanna see that lovely eye
Contact I don't get jealous, I'm a very nice guy
You just make me so crazy I'd like to apply
Your makeup just to watch someone finish and magnify
The image I love your sensual nature and I
Simply feel like your body makes mine glorify
I wish you'd send me a picture with a creampie
If I had one job I'd work for the FBI
Female body inspector and I'm super sly
The tears I'm talking about don't come from my eye

# FACE

She really wants to twerk on my face
She's wearing something red hot and lace
She says sir please would you replace
My fingers with your face
She wants me to take her to outer space
She loves on my face to pick up the pace
She squirts everywhere when she shakes
I drink her juices, love the taste
Princess I advise to start to brace
Yourself I've got a load of unicorn paste
That I'm going to cover your face
With as my mouth and her pussy embrace
She's grabbing me dick with great haste
She keeps grinding her sexy waist
I'm beating it up, neighbors like murder was the case
She's a beautiful rose and I'm a vase
I want you to put your flower right on my face

# FEISTY

She was calm until  she became feisty
You'll never see it if you treat her rightly
But if you disrespect her enough you'll find a mighty
Strong force that will yell mightily
Most don't expect someone so tiny
To be so forceful and so feisty
She'll be feisty when she's ninety
Her sense of humor is subtle, she dryly
States funny things then smiles slyly
I made sure to tie her down tightly
She's extra mad and screaming fight me
I love when she's saucy and fiery
There's something in her voice that's so spicy
Nothing gets me going like when she's feisty

# FILING

In my dreams you spent the whole night filing
You did your best to interrupt my typing
Your skirt just slowly rising
As I am unable to focus, this distraction I'm fighting
You look back at me coyly smiling
You questions why the bottom cabinet always need filing
Today you have a secret you have been hiding
You bent over in the middle of my check signing
I swear it was like my body was struck by lightning
No panties today you are really trying
 To get a raise my eyebrows aren't the only things rising
My sexy secretary is absolutely mesmerizing
Sat on my lap as I whisper I'm hiring
You an assistant, bring a friend, you're both filing

# FINGERING

She enjoyed it most his considering
Getting her the hottest of it's blistering
Her body started sweating it's simmering
That's when I slowly start whispering
The naughtiest things she's listening
Carefully she slyly started fingering
Herself and says is this what you're picturing
My tongue on her thighs she starts whimpering
Her body shakes like she's shivering
It was wild and quite bewildering
How the intense pleasure I'm delivering
She's reading this and it's glistening
I love watching her horny fingering

# Fire Tornado

He started speaking deeply and slow
He spoke saying as above so below
He described a peony filled meadow
He was the wind and started to blow
Her petals and his smooth tempo
Created a dazzling fire tornado
His words made her soul brightly glow
In a world as cold as snow
He helped her flames overflow
She said I think you deserve to know
That you dear sir, you're a total pro
At pleasing me when you start to follow
Up your words by sucking on my big toe
You make the most intense fire tornado

# FOCUSED

She knew she had to be focused
With me I focused my trust
I whisper you create so much lust
Fuck you did it again I cussed
Dreaming of you playing with my nuts
Slow down, there's no need to rush
Staring at my lap you're quite focused
I know you know how to get an A plus
Come to the back of the school bus
Your tutor is ready to make you blush
On your knees, begging me to bust
I'm going to rearrange your guts
My nuts in your mouth, I'm quite focused

# FOR PLAY

She invited me over for play
I suggested she relax and lay
Back, tell me everything that brings dismay
I start massaging her scalp saying hey
She said I'm really enjoying the way
You are so thoughtful you may
Explore my body anyway
That you desire the care you display
Gets me very heated, I pray
That my tongue is able to convey
My desire to melt your problems away
Your thighs are my favorite entrée
Your breasts are a magnificent display
Of divinity your ass is gourmet
Do you enjoy the way I portray
Your beauty is this excellent foreplay
Do I light your fire with hot wordplay
I'm molding your pleasure like clay
Custom poetry for your birthday
I look forward to coming over for play

# FOREVER

We are truly friends forever
One thing constant, that will never
Change is we never criticize or lecture
We just like having fun and pleasure
When skies are stormy and the weather
Is rough we hug firmly together
How does it get better than my friend in leather
I dunno sometimes I'm simply not clever
Enough to answer she's like wondering whether
I'm wearing panties today she's like have you ever
Seen something so beautiful it makes my blood pressure
And other things rise; for her I'm hard forever

# Freaking Lovely

It's quite ironic and very funny
That she said my words are freaking lovely
She's wild, fierce, and she
Well she's really freaking lovely
She's golden and sweeter than honey
A mermaid that frolics in the turquoise sea
She is more exotic than a plumeria tree
She's a wild jungle Barbie
Climbing out the forest naked, with a machete
She elevates and alters my reality
She's absolutely amazing, freaking lovely
Especially her dynamic, soulful personality
She's the embodiment of sensuality
She's a torch ginger and I'm a bumblebee
I'm pollinating her mind, that's freaking lovely

# FREAKING

Today a poem about when she starts freaking
Out I do things to her that she can't start speaking
Fuck sir seriously I'm leaking
My tongue slides in and she starts shrieking
Under your desk I'm carefully sneaking
She's so turned on by my delicious teasing
My fingers make her start squeaking
Sir please don't ever stop eating
Me so hotly this wetness has her really freaking
I give her just what she is needing
She's touching herself while reading
These words and her body starts screaming
For more he likes when she starts excreting
Her juices I'm licking her while she's sleeping
When she's chilly I'm her heating
Under the covers her hands start creeping
She can't help herself she's squeezing
Her breasts saying sir you are freaking
Amazing I love how you keep treating
Me to yummy deliciousness am I leaving
A puddle again her essence is seeping
Everywhere she's like I must be dreaming

# FRISKIEST

What's gotten into that kitten, it's the friskiest
She put on her makeup and the skimpiest
Outfit and some very sexy fishnets
Eat a sandwich kitten you're the skinniest
She's rubbing against my legs, she's the friendliest
Kitten leaving a puddle she's the drippiest
She's very excited, she's sticking out, she's the nippiest
She is being super forward, she's the friendliest
Kitten her texts are truly the silliest
She's rubbing herself, she's the squishiest
Her hips and mouth are the busiest
My kitten is definitely the kinkiest
I'm covered in her excitement, she's the milkiest
She purrs when I say she's the prettiest
Thing my kitten's mouth is doing the riskiest
Things she's the naughtiest kitten, she's friskiest

# Gentleman

She found herself alone with a gentleman
Normally nice men were so bland
But when he spoke deeply excuse me ma'am
I can tell most men try to command
You and me well I'm a gentleman
She leaned back as he kissed her hand
He spoke saying your beauty is greater than
Any I've ever seen before, you are quite grand
Her temperature raised and he started to fan
Her as he channeled her attention span
His nature increased her wingspan
Normally I'm a total gentleman
But you've made it impossible to stand
I'm a sinner and I'll be damned
If you haven't made me greatly expand
She watched as his eyes hotly scanned
Her body and saying I've found the promised land
He gently revealed he was no gentleman
She got on her knees saying I understand
She swallowed him whole, he gasped muttering I'll be goddamned

# GENTLY

He treats her sweetly and gently
Being adored and respected feels heavenly
He whispers the naughtiest things pleasantly
It gets her excited and boy did she
Enjoy a lover that was super gentlemanly
He desires her pleasure and whispers we
Are opening our hearts safely and carefree
His tongue was her favorite gift under the Christmas tree
He rubbed her feet firmly and her glee
Increased sometimes she enjoys saying not gently
Please go harder, he was her cup of tea
She feels so hot it alters her reality

# GOOD FRIEND

She says I'm an angel, such a good friend
But I hesitate sometimes to press send
She says I'm a blessing, a godsend
In my dreams she slowly starts to bend
Over and my dick starts to extend
You love making me hard good friend
Do I speak freely or do I pretend
That I want my tongue in your rear end
I know I don't wish to offend
Her but I woke up dreaming this weekend
With her offering me her mouth to lend
Me her holes can she comprehend
I don't need or want a girlfriend
Just a really slutty good friend

# GRINDING

You're in my lap and you start slowly grinding
On my dick you fast forward and then keep rewinding
You let me grab, you aren't minding
The attention I'm striking your clit like lightning
Surrender bitch there's no use in fighting
You love getting juicy from my writing
I make your body happy and shining
Touch yourself and you'll be finding
New sensations and the pleasures will be spell binding
And the colors will be blinding
I know right now you can't help sliding
Your fingers in, I know you are grinding

# HEELS

She looks the dopest in heels
I wear that type of beauty heals
Me and inspires all the feels
She's rolling over the competition with wheels
Ludacris cue Roll Out and let's steal
Her heart by keeping it totally real
Miss you've got the sexiest heels
I'll just keep her laughing let's make a deal
I'll prepare the most elegant meal
And you'll wear your sexiest heels
She embodies sex appeal
I'll do anything to please her with great zeal
Looking at her in heels gets me as hard as steel

# HIKING

She loves when I speak about how exciting
She found my attitude so inviting
I knew just how to make her start hiking
 Her skirt up she couldn't stop my writing
Was so pleasurable, just to her liking
She gasps as my focus on lightening
Her burden an angel that's trying
To go to hell like hey how about tying
You up blindfolded and licking you striking
Your mind and fingers start sliding
Over your thighs there's no hiding
The puddle left on my lightning
Rod I' her mountain and she's climbing
Right onto this deliciousness we're hiking

# HONORABLE

She had never felt so worthy and honorable
I said you can do anything, you are able
Building her up she's no princess in a fable
She's queen of the jungle her beauty is fatal
I mean she's drop dead gorgeous that's my label
She inspires me to act lovingly and honorable
Together in a storm we feel stable
Holding each other and I'm pretty playful
I wish she'd sit her ass on the table
And let me start licking her navel
I have a thought that's way less than honorable
I wonder how she feels about anal
Spreading her ass like it's a bagel
Cream cheese everywhere I'm unable
To contain myself my pants have become unstable

# HOTTER MESS

I wanted to sweetly think of a way to express
Like the opportunity to fully address
Your physical needs let me ease your stress
You playfully let me look up your dress
As you slowly start saying more sweetness yes
I'm here to heal and bless
Your heart; most want your clothing to become less
I like you clothed and I must confess
I dream of making a hot mess a hotter mess
Whispering perhaps you should start to caress
Yourself, grateful for someone who would always obsess
About giving you pleasure I want to give you rest
I want to pleasure you and impress
You by letting you authentically express
Your needs and wants treating you with great kindness
Saying may I please serve you my highness
May I make you experience the opposite of dryness
Was my attempt to make you wet a success
Did I just make you an even hotter mess?

# I Love Itttttt

She gave into temptation saying I love ittttt
I want to make you leave a mark where you sit
Screenshotting my poetry because it gets
You leaking let me lick your unicorn mist
Let me slowly start nibbling your hips
Does this get you going, are you biting your lip
Does this make your fire get really lit
Show me those amazing perfect tits
Why don't you drool on them, show me some spit
I've got the secret ingredient for your banana split
Spread your legs and I'll make you emit
So much moistness drown me in your juices I love ittttt!

# ICE

She's fiery hot and I'm her vice
I tempt her with her biggest vice
She is really turned on by being treated nice
I use ice cubes and my tongue and the most precise
Spots she calls it her paradise
She's a wild cat and I'm a gang of mice
Eeeeeeek she's like seriously I just came twice
I'm making her see colors like the Northern Lights
I muzzle that cat cause she bites
I know the thing that really excites
Her is when I use lots of spice
Oh sir I have now come thrice
We're going to need another bucket of ice

# IMPERFECTIONS

You truly have the most beautiful imperfections
You've shown me what true love is, it's a great lesson
I build you up and never lessen
My support I always share vulnerable affection
Exposing my heart and knowing your imperfections
Would never harm me and you've got the prettiest imperfections
You've got the best hair, breasts, lips, and midsection
You've got such an extensive fancy lingerie collection
Nobody is perfect, there's no such things as perfection
But very close is your super sexy reflection
I reflect you, we have a very special connection
For you I care most for your safety and protection
I'll protect your heart and ask great questions
Like have I told you lately how much I admire your imperfections?

# INCREDIBLE

He dreams of making her feel incredible
He did things that most found unacceptable
But the naughtier he was, the more delectable
He was to her she whispers you're terrible
He carefully and discreetly climbs under the table
His tongue so long and super flexible
If he keeps it up there will be a spectacle
His kisses were feathery light and plentiful
She felt her body's pleasure in multi-dimensional
Ways he dragged her inside of a confessional
And made her drip on his face like caramel
He smiled and said your taste is impeccable
Nobody had ever made her feel so sensual
Being treated sweetly and put on a pedestal
Healed her soul, his touch was healing and medical
Her anticipation aroused the strongest chemicals
In her brain and the way his tongue was on her genitals
Well she often finds her speechless, it's incredible!

# INDEED

I whisper the hottest things she needs
More wetness oh and there it is indeed
She likes when I bite her hard enough to bleed
She loves when we do the deed
She's a dog in heat and ready to breed
She swallows my dick with such greed
She's touching herself as she starts to read
Oh my goodness so much wetness indeed
She like it firm and with lots of speed
Did I get it juicy for your baby, did I succeed
Of course I did, you're super wet now indeed

# INSISTENCE

She loved when I provide her assistance
She said make me super wet her insistence
She needed wetness right now, this instant
Mumbling Jesus Christ but she's not religious
She gave into temptation with no resistance
She's a ho ho ho not just on Christmas
She's the hottest devil in existence
I make her leak with great persistence
Touch yourself hotly at my insistence

# INTERVIEW

I'm supposed to focus on this interview
All I can think about is your hot shoe
Rubbing my lap and I'm bulging through
My pants um sir excuse you
This is a professional interview
Thinking of you my bulge really grew
I can't stop making lots of glue
Thinking of you in see through
Clothes you bring at the zoo
In me picturing you when you blew
Me away by swallowing my goo
You make absolutely nothing taboo
I can't believe you started to screw
Yourself I'm having déjà vu
You've made me mess up another interview

# KITTEN

On Frisky Friday we pet our kitten
OMG is that a bag of ribbons
Kitten is so cute, everyone is smitten
Play with your kitten and listen
Nothing is off limits with these women
They say play with your cock, don't be chicken
Jesus Christ isn't the only thing that's risen
Frisky Friday let's do what's totally forbidden
Your kitten has a singular purpose, one mission
Frisky kitten wants to make your cat glisten
I'm bending you over in the kitchen
My tongue is frantic, nobody has ever given
You such good head frisky kitten
You can feel me start to stiffen
I'm staining your dress like Bill Clinton
My lust for you can't be hidden
You drive me wild and I'm driven
To make you absolutely slippin
Give into temptation, give into sin
Pet your kitty and pet your kitten

# Kitty

She really enjoys men that are witty
A great personality is a really
Big turn on I think she's super pretty
She shakes her ass and it makes me dizzy
She's bending over in a skirt that's mini
Oh my goodness she just flashed me her kitty
It appears I've made her quite wet and sticky
She wants it fast, she needs it quickly
Please sir, please stick it in me
Her hands are so fast and busy
She's curvaceous yet skinny
I'm her Kermit and she's my Miss Piggy
She's reading this and touching her kitty

# LATE

She is predictable, always late
I know good things come to those that wait
She always has time to feel great
She reads this and can anticipate
That he's naughty and she's like I'm late
I say just a second as I help her locate
Her panties she will donate
Them to me as I take her whole weight
On my lap she's not on a date
She's using me to help her masturbate
She needs it now, she needs it at eight
She's bending over and my tongue creates
Lots of pleasure, I'm the reason the playmate
Is consistently running late

# LEARNING

I am her teacher and she isn't learning
I spank her ass hard until it starts burning
She sucked on her lollipop she was flirting
She opened her legs and could tell it was working
Oh a lesson in pain she's earning
I could tell her greatest yearning
The first spank she started squirming
Bad bitch I knew it was hurting
Her butt and it was really turning
Her on a really hard spank and she starts squirming
Her juices go everywhere; the puddle is forming
How wet can she get, we are still learning

# LET'S HAVE SOME FUN

Sliding into your DMs whispering let's have some fun
I know how to really stun
You girl your body is banging like a machine gun
You are single but you are hitting homeruns
Ladies first you will be totally satisfied before I have begun
Get your hair done, put on something cute, let's have some fun
Let me feed you chocolate and fresh fruit while I rub your bum
You deserve to be worshipped, let me be that someone
Picture yourself lying on the Maui sands soaking in the sun
Let's get to know each, let's have some fun

# Librarian

She's dressing sexily like a librarian
She's a sick puppy and I'm her veterinarian
She's smacking me with her ruler, sexy authoritarian
I'm grabbing her hair like a barbarian
She's sexy Catwoman and I'm Batman
I'm collecting her juices with a drip pan
She's melting all over her favorite snowman
Today I showed up dressed like a clergyman
She's an atomic bomb and I'm Japan
I predict a flash flood, I'm her weatherman
With jokes like Will Ferrel in Anchorman
How does it get better than a sexy librarian
She's an open book and I've got a plan
Today she's filing in the bottom drawer my sexitarian
Isn't wearing any panties today I'm her hitman
I'm sliding all the way in my librarian

# LICK

She laid back and let him lick
Her she needed it and she wanted it quick
He knows how to get her very slick
He's her favorite toy, her pogo stick
She's touching herself thinking of my thick
Cock down her throat she loves my dick
Holding her down firmly I lick
Her tight pussy, her legs start to kick
Filming another naughty little flick
She's my filthiest, nastiest chick
My dick is totally covered in her lipstick
She love when I let her lick

# LIGHTERS

We aren't lovers, we are lighters
Together we are making light at a higher
Level she's a very wild tiger
And she looks at my meat with great desire
She said you're the horniest writer
I know just how to light her fire
She's moaning and is quite hyper
I'm electric and she's my live wire
She says your vulnerability gives me great desire
She feels her body becoming lighter
My tongue, it never seems to tire
My wild tiger is a ferocious biter
She got her stripes from playing with lighters

# LISTENING

Few men spend their time really listening
I pay careful attention to make sure I am giving
My full attention what are you wishing
For if it's pleasure I'm dishing
Out things that make you start listening
I know just how to keep you glistening
Start by exclaiming you're so interesting
My tongue's pace starts quickening
I make her act like a whore she's not soliciting
She's just a total freak she starts pinching
Her nipples her body feels riveting
A river of pleasure as you start swiveling
Nothing gets you wetter than superior listening

# Lonely

She touched herself a lot, she was lonely
She needed his fire to feel cozy
She loved how he acted boldly
His patience and desire unfolded slowly
She loved his deep voice, he would lowly
Whisper let my tongue make you forget being lonely
She fucks me like she wants a trophy
We're so far away but fucking closely
I keep making her say fucking hell holy
Shit he's making me cum remotely
She thinks of me when she gets lonely

# MANIFEST

She said playfully guess what I manifest
I laughingly replied is this a test
She said come on guess
I said might I suggest
That I help you get it off your chest
Wait I mean get off on your chest are you undressed
Being naughty is what you do best
Guess what you made me manifest
She's getting warmer as I expressed
Myself did you dream you're under arrest
Or just handcuffed and you should invest
In learning to be totally blessed
My tongue on your body I'm obsessed
With your pleasure I want to be the best
Wear emerald green cowboy boots playing wild west
Giddy up cowgirl let me relieve your stressed
Body with my tongue will leave you unstressed
A friend with benefits is that your wish to manifest?

# Meeting

She felt lucky at our chance meeting
I threw her over my shoulder she's leaving
With me I love that she's never speaking
I'd much rather see her leaking
Dripping on me and totally relieving
Her stress she grins little devil is sneaky
If you excite her enough she gets squeaky
Let me worship your body completely
Lay back and beg please eat me
Your body and my tongue will have an extended meeting
My words breathe fire in your soul I'm heating
You up amazing what politely treating
A lady does I picture you excreting
Your volcanic explosions keep you overheating
Baby am I the reason your fingers and body keep meeting?

# MESMERIZING

Tonight I met one of the most mesmerizing
Creatures she's absolutely electrifying
She's so pretty my dick starts crying
I want to be continuously mesmerizing
Let me say your body is redefining
You make me hard quicker than lightning
You're wet like flowers in the spring
I want to please you, make you sing
My praises with your juices I'm dying
To taste your ass I bet it taste mesmerizing

# MODESTY

She likes to outwardly show her modesty
He knew how to get her neurology
To let her forget her psychology
Back to her nature, back to biology
She practiced her racy photography
With him and there was little modesty
She was a hot tease without any apology
Together they came up with a great policy
They created hot, unique artistry
Super racy and discrete was their policy
She loved having someone to pose hotly
For and she treasured his honesty
She wondered if perhaps he possibly
Would enjoy her acting immodestly
They made are of the highest quality